EMMA
Every Day

Tap Dance Troubles

by C.L. Reid

illustrated by Elena Aiello

PICTURE WINDOW BOOKS
a capstone imprint

Emma Every Day is published by
Picture Window Books, an imprint of Capstone
1710 Roe Crest Drive, North Mankato, Minnesota 56003
www.capstonepub.com

Library of Congress Cataloging-in-Publication Data
Names: Reid, C.L., author. | Aiello, Elena (Illustrator), illustrator.
Title: Tap dance troubles / by C.L. Reid ; illustrated by Elena Aiello.
Description: North Mankato, MN : Picture Window Books, 2020. |
Series: Emma every day | Audience: Ages 5-7.

Summary: Emma is taking tap dance lessons, and she wants to learn the
routine perfectly, but it is not easy because the tapping of the dancers
makes it difficult for her Cochlear Implant to pick up the final notes
of the music and so her timing is off—but with a little help from her
teacher and her best friend, Izzie, Emma will make it work. Includes an
ASL fingerspelling chart, glossary, and content-related questions.

Identifiers: LCCN 2020001366 (print) | LCCN 2020001367 (ebook) |
ISBN 9781515871811 (hardcover) | ISBN 9781515873129 (paperback) |
ISBN 9781515871897 (adobe pdf)

Subjects: LCSH: Deaf children—Juvenile fiction. | Tap dancing—Juvenile
fiction. | Cochlear implants—Juvenile fiction. | Best friends—Juvenile
fiction. | Persistence—Juvenile fiction. | CYAC: Deaf—Fiction. | People
with disabilities—Fiction. | Tap dancing—Fiction. | Dance—Fiction. | Best
friends—Fiction. | Friendship—Fiction. | Persistence—Fiction.

Classification: LCC PZ7.1.R4544 Tap 2020 (print) |
LCC PZ7.1.R4544 (ebook) | DDC [E]—dc23
LC record available at https://lccn.loc.gov/2020001366
LC ebook record available at https://lccn.loc.gov/2020001367

Image Credits: Capstone: Daniel Griffo, 29 top, Randy Chewning, 28,
Margeaux Lucas, 29 bottom right, Michael Reid, 29 bottom left
Design Elements: Shutterstock: achii, Mari C, Mika Besfamilnaya

Designer: Tracy McCabe

TABLE OF CONTENTS

MEET EMMA

EMMA CARTER
Age: 8 Grade: 3

SIBLING
One brother, Jaden
(12 years old)

PARENTS
David and Lucy

BEST FRIEND
Izzie Jackson

PET
a goldfish named Ruby

favorite color: teal
favorite food: tacos
favorite school subject: writing
favorite sport: swimming
hobbies: reading, writing, biking, swimming

FINGERSPELLING GUIDE

MANUAL ALPHABET

Aa   Bb   Cc   Dd   Ee

Ff   Gg   Hh   Ii   Jj

MANUAL NUMBERS

0   1   2   3

Emma is Deaf. She uses American Sign Language (ASL) to communicate with her family. She also uses a Cochlear Implant (CI) to help her hear.

Kk Ll Mm Nn Oo

Pp Qq Rr Ss Tt Uu

Vv Ww Xx Yy Zz

Chapter 1
Tap, Tap, Tap

"Time to move the rug

again," Emma signed to her dad.

He rolled it up. Then he moved

out of the way so Emma could

dance. Her dance show was in

a few days.

Click. Clack. Tap, tap, tap. Emma worked hard. She touched her Cochlear Implant (CI) to make sure it wouldn't fall off. Then she practiced some more.

The song drew to an end. She spun around and posed.

Mom and Dad clapped. Jaden gave her a thumbs-up.

"Wow!"  Dad fingerspelled.

"Wonderful!" Mom signed.

Emma wiped sweat off her face.

"Thanks. I want to do my very best," she signed.

Emma had just started a dance class. She didn't want to make any mistakes at the show.

But as Emma got ready for bed, the worries snuck in. Whenever she was worried, Emma talked to her pet fish, Ruby.

"Will I make mistakes at the show? Will I be able to hear the music okay?" she asked Ruby.

Ruby just kept swimming in circles. She wasn't much help.

Chapter 2
The Spin

At dance class the next day,
everyone was excited. Miss Judith
held up a hand to quiet the room.

"The show is this Saturday. Let's
get to work," Miss Judith said.

The music started. *Click. Clack. Tap, tap, tap.* As the music drew to an end, everyone spun around and posed.

Everyone except Emma. She couldn't hear the final notes of the song.

"That was good, but let's try it again," Miss Judith said.

The music started over. *Click.*

Clack. Tap, tap, tap. The tapping

of the shoes was too loud. Emma

couldn't hear the music.

At the end of the song, Emma

didn't spin with the others.

"Emma, what's wrong?" Miss

Judith asked.

"The tapping of the shoes is too loud. I can't hear the music," Emma said.

"Remember to count your dance steps," Miss Judith replied. "We do everything in counts of eight. Just keep counting to eight. You can do it!"

"I can tap Emma's arm when it's time to spin," Izzie said.

Emma liked that plan. She also changed the program on her CI. That would make the background noises quieter.

"Cool,"  Miss Judith fingerspelled. "Let's try again."

Izzie stood next to Emma and held her thumb up.

The music started. *Click. Clack. Tap, tap, tap.* Emma focused. She counted to eight over and over.

As the song ended, Izzie touched Emma's arm. Emma spun around and posed with the rest of the class.

"Very good!" Miss Judith clapped her hands.

Emma smiled. She started to feel a lot better.

Chapter 3

Showtime!

Click. Clack. Tap, tap, tap. It was

the night before the dance show.

Emma was back in her living room

practicing.

Emma counted to eight over and over again. The song ended. Emma spun around and posed.

"You'll do great tomorrow," Dad signed.

A big smile spread across Emma's face.

"Yes, I think I will," she signed. Then she headed to bed.

The day was finally here. Emma

packed her bag.  She

stretched. She put on her costume.

She was ready to go!

The dancers lined up on the stage. Emma changed the program on her CI. Then she took a deep breath and smiled.

The music started. So did the tapping. *Click. Clack. Tap, tap, tap.*

Emma counted to eight over and over. The song was almost done. She waited for Izzie to tap her arm. But that didn't happen.

Emma didn't worry. She kept counting and dancing.

One, two, three, four, five, six, seven, eight. Then she spun around with the others and posed. The audience cheered.

"Sorry I forgot to tap you," Izzie signed.

"That's okay," Emma signed. "I did it all on my own. I love to dance!"

LEARN TO SIGN

mother

Touch thumb to chin.

father

Touch thumb to forehead.

brother

1. Place thumb on forehead.
2. Bring wrists together.

sister

1. Slide thumb along cheek.
2. Bring wrists together.

excited

Bend middle fingers and make small circles at chest.

applause

Twist hands near face.

dance

Move fingers back and forth on palm.

music

Move hand back and forth along arm.

GLOSSARY

Cochlear Implant (also called CI)—a device that helps someone who is Deaf to hear; it is worn on the head just above the ear

communicate—to pass along thoughts, feelings, or information

deaf—being unable to hear

fingerspell—to make letters with your hands to spell out words; often used for names of people and places

focus—keep all your attention on one thing

nervous—feeling worried or anxious

pose—to keep your body in a set position

sign—use hand gestures to communicate

sign language—a language in which hand gestures, along with facial expressions and body movements, are used instead of speech

TALK ABOUT IT

1. Emma loves to dance. What do you love to do? Use the fingerspelling guide at the beginning of the book to sign your favorite hobby.

2. Emma has to work hard to learn her dance. Talk about a time you had to practice something over and over.

3. Dance isn't easy for Emma. Why do you think she sticks with it?

WRITE ABOUT IT

1. Pretend you are Emma. Write a paragraph about your dance show.

2. Emma has a great dance teacher. Make a list of things you think makes a great teacher.

3. Write a few sentences about your favorite hobby.

Ruby

ABOUT THE AUTHOR

Deaf-blind since childhood, C.L. Reid received a Cochlear Implant (CI) as an adult to help her hear, and she uses American Sign Language (ASL) to communicate. She and her husband have three sons. Their middle son is also deaf-blind. Reid earned a master's degree in writing for children and young adults at Hamline University in St. Paul, Minnesota. Reid lives in Minnesota with her husband, two of their sons, and their cats.

ABOUT THE ILLUSTRATOR

Elena Aiello is an illustrator and character designer. After graduating as a marketing specialist, she decided to study art direction and CGI. Doing so, she discovered a passion for illustration and conceptual art. She works as a freelancer for various magazines and publishers. Elena loves video games and sushi and lives with her husband and her little pug, Gordon, in Milan, Italy.